"Like, watch this, Scoob," Shaggy said. They were in the back of the Mystery Machine. "Here's a little trick I got from that magician we saw on TV last night."

Shaggy picked up an empty paper plate. He held it on the palm of his hand. Then he took a red handkerchief out of his back pocket and waved it in the air.

"Notice this ordinary handkerchief," Shaggy said. "I will now put it over this ordinary paper plate."

Shaggy covered the plate with the handkerchief. He waved his hand over it three times.

"Abracadabra, me-oh-my-oh," Shaggy chanted. "Make this plate a pizza pie-o."

Shaggy whisked the handkerchief off the plate in a flash. The plate was still a plate.

"Shaggy, you can't just say some words and expect magic to happen," Fred said. "It takes years to learn how to make things appear and disappear."

"If that's true, Shaggy and Scooby *have* been magicians for years," Daphne said.

"What are you talking about?" Velma asked.

"Who else can make a whole pizza disappear right before your eyes?" Daphne asked, smiling.

Everyone in the van laughed.

"Technically, there's no such thing as magic," Velma said.

"Of course there is, Velma," Daphne said.

"No, there isn't," replied Velma. "There's a logical explanation for every magic trick you see."

Written by
James Gelsey

A
LITTLE APPLE
PAPERBACK

SCHOLASTIC INC.
New York   Toronto   London   Auckland   Sydney
Mexico City   New Delhi   Hong Kong

For David and Emily

No part of this work may be reproduced, stored in a retrieval system, or transmitted in any form or by any means, electronic, mechanical, photocopying, recording, or otherwise, without written permission of the publisher. For information regarding permission, write to Scholastic Inc., Attention: Permissions Department, 555 Broadway, New York, NY 10012.

ISBN 0-439-18878-4

12 11   3 4 5 6/0

Printed in the U.S.A.
First Scholastic printing, January 2001

"Well, I like not knowing the logical explanations," Daphne said. "It's more fun that way."

Fred steered the Mystery Machine into a parking lot. "Here we are, gang," he said. "The Magic Palace."

Fred parked the van in a spot right up front, and the gang got out. They were all dressed formally, in black and white. They were going to help out at a charity benefit that evening.

Above them towered the Magic Palace, where the benefit was being held. It was made of stone and had a big front door that looked like a drawbridge. A row of towers lined the top of the building.

"Jinkies," Velma said. "It looks just like a castle."

"Right out of a storybook," added Daphne. "How wonderful!"

3

"Like, it looks kinda creepy to me," Shaggy said. "Maybe Scooby and I will wait for you in the Mystery Machine." They turned to go back into the van.

"Oh, no, you don't," Daphne replied. "We're here to help out at the charity benefit tonight. And then we'll get to watch the magic show."

"Who knows, Shaggy, maybe you'll even learn some real magic," Fred said.

"Like how to make a pizza appear?" asked Shaggy.

"Rizza! Rum!" barked Scooby. He and Shaggy looked at each other.

"Okay, okay, you talked us into it," Shaggy said.

The gang walked up the front path toward the enormous door. But before Fred could reach out and turn the doorknob, the door slowly creaked open.

"Zoinks!" Shaggy exclaimed. "This place isn't haunted, is it?"

"Of course not, Shaggy," Daphne said. "It's just a magic door."

"Actually, the door opened because we stepped on a pressure-sensitive plate beneath the walkway," Velma explained. "There was nothing magical about it."

The gang walked through a very small and dark entryway. They passed through another doorway and into a dark room.

"That's strange," Fred said. "There doesn't seem to be anyone here."

"Like, are you sure the benefit is tonight, Daph?" asked Shaggy.

"Of course I'm sure," Daphne replied. She looked around a bit. "At least, I think so."

A strange voice suddenly pierced the darkness.

"Abracadabra!" it shouted. Then — FLASH! — all of the lights came on. The gang was standing in a giant ballroom. An enormous chandelier hung from the ceiling above their heads.

"Welcome to the Magic Palace!" the voice said.

Chapter 2

The gang looked around. The enormous chandelier provided all of the light in the giant, circular ballroom. Its curved walls were covered with large portraits and tapestries.

"It looks like all of these people in the pictures are magicians," Daphne said. "Look, there's Harry Houdini."

She pointed to a portrait of Harry Houdini. He was hanging upside down inside a giant tank of water. He was wearing a straitjacket and several chains were wrapped around his body.

"Man, that's some bathing suit," Shaggy said. He and Scooby giggled.

"That looks like a portrait of Merlin the Magician," Velma said. In the picture, Merlin was wearing a pointy cap with stars and planets shimmering on it.

"Like, what's with the bathrobe?" Shaggy asked. "Did he just get out of bed or something?" He and Scooby giggled again.

"Merlin lived a long time ago," Velma said. "In the days of King Arthur. People dressed differently then."

"I wonder who that is," Fred said. He pointed to a large portrait of a woman dressed in a golden gown. She wore a beautiful diamond necklace.

"It is I, Eudora Pillbox, of course," said the woman in the portrait.

"Rikes!" Scooby barked, jumping into Shaggy's arms.

The woman in the portrait stepped forward. Her right foot came out of the picture frame and

reached down to touch the ballroom floor. But then she lost her balance and tumbled right out of the picture frame onto the floor.

"Are you all right?" Daphne asked as the gang rushed over.

The woman was laughing. "Oh, yes, I'm fine," she said. Then she reached up and touched the diamond necklace. "Thank goodness," she said. "Wouldn't want anything to happen to this. We're auctioning it off at the end of the night. It's worth a lot of money, you know."

Fred and Daphne helped the woman stand up.

"Please forgive my little joke," she said. "I know it wasn't very nice, but I had to try it out on someone before the guests arrive. It's my favorite trick in this ballroom. You must be the kids who are helping with the charity event."

"That's right," Fred said. "I'm Fred. And this is Daphne, Velma, Shaggy, and Scooby-Doo."

"Thank you all for coming tonight," Eudora said. "And welcome to the Magic Palace."

"Like, that voice sounds familiar," Shaggy

said. "Hey, do you work at the Hungry Hobo drive-through window?"

"Shaggy!" Daphne scolded. "Ms. Pillbox was the one who said 'Abracadabra' before the lights went on."

"That's right, Daphne," Eudora replied. "And please, everyone, call me Eudora. Now, this is a very special night for me. The Masked Magician is going to be performing!"

"The Masked Magician? He's the best magician in the world," Fred said. "I'm sure your benefit is going to be a huge success."

"I hope so," Eudora said sadly. "If anything goes wrong tonight, my reputation will

be ruined. The fact is, I've been getting some mysterious notes ever since I announced the benefit."

"What kind of notes?" Velma asked.

"Notes warning me something terrible will happen tonight," Eudora answered.

"Rikes!" Scooby gulped.

"Like, that goes double for me," Shaggy whispered.

"But I can't let some silly notes bother me now," Eudora said. "Here's what I need you to do. Daphne, you can help me welcome the guests. Fred and Velma, I'd like you to help make sure people don't get lost. The rooms here are not always what they seem to be. And Shaggy and Scooby, I need you to work in the coatroom. Any questions?"

"Like, just one," Shaggy said. "How do we get there?"

The gang looked around and realized that there were no doors leading into or out of the ballroom. They couldn't even find the one they'd entered through!

"That's one of the wonderful things about the Magic Palace," Eudora said. "Things are never as they appear."

"Like the picture you stepped out of?" Daphne asked.

"Exactly, my dear," said Eudora. "The coatroom is to the right of Merlin. The main entrance is next to Houdini. And the hall to the dining room is right over there." She pointed to a wall on the other side of the ballroom.

"Open sesame," Eudora chanted. Doorways magically lit up behind the pictures on the walls. Then the pictures rolled up into the ceiling like window shades.

"Jinkies," Velma said. "I guess this really is a magic palace."

Shaggy and Scooby walked toward the door to the coatroom. "If only we could make some food appear as easily as Eudora did with the doors," Shaggy said. "Now, *that* would be magic."

"Reah, ragic," Scooby agreed.

"Be careful, you two," Velma called from across the ballroom.

"What do you mean, Velma?" Shaggy called back. "We're only going to the coatroom. What kind of trouble could we possibly cause there?"

Chapter 3

 haggy and Scooby sat inside the coatroom. There were lots and lots of empty
metal hangers. Shaggy reached up and
grabbed one, then balanced it on his nose.

"Well, Scoob, if Fred, Velma, and Daphne
ask what we did tonight," Shaggy said, "we
can honestly tell them all we did was hang
around. Get it? Hang around? Hangers?" He
and Scooby laughed.

"Ahem," someone said outside the coatroom.

"Hey, it's our first customer," Shaggy said.

"Let's get to work." He and Scooby jumped up and raced to the door.

"It's about time," said the man who was standing there. He was dressed in a black tuxedo and wore a black cape over his shoulders.

"Hey, aren't you Muldoon the Magnificent?" Shaggy asked.

A slight smile crept across the man's lips. "Yes, I am he," he said.

"Man, Scooby and I love watching your TV specials," Shaggy gushed. "We especially liked last night's show where you made a whole nine-course dinner appear out of nowhere."

Muldoon's smile grew larger. "Yes, that was good, wasn't it?" he asked. "And not a

16

drop of soup spilled. Perfection, if I do say so myself."

"I wonder if the Masked Magician will do something like that tonight?" Shaggy asked Scooby.

"Ri ron't row," Scooby said with a shrug.

"You know, I was supposed to tape a special television performance for the benefit. It was going to be broadcast here tonight," Muldoon said. "It was arranged months ago. And I planned to do the whole 'magic banquet' bit. This time it was going to be a twelve-course dinner."

Shaggy's and Scooby's mouths hung open. They both licked their lips.

"I was even going to add a special ending where I turn a banana tree and a cow into a giant banana cream pie," continued Muldoon. "But then Eudora Pillbox told me she wanted a live performance and hired the Masked Magician to perform instead. Believe me, she'll never do that to Muldoon the

Magnificent again!" Muldoon turned and started to stalk away.

"Uh, like, Mr. Magnificent?" Shaggy called. "Do you want to leave your cape?"

Muldoon stopped, turned around, and walked back to the coatroom. He took off his cape and handed it to Shaggy.

"Thank you," he said. Then he stormed off again.

"That's too bad about the banana cream pie," Shaggy said. "I sure could use something like that right now."

"How about an apple, son?" asked a man who was walking up to the coatroom. He took a red silk handkerchief out of his breast pocket. Then he made a fist with his other hand and stuffed the handkerchief into it.

18

"Hocus-pocus!" the man said. "And, *voilà!*" He opened his hand and showed Shaggy and Scooby a small red apple. "Here you go."

"Thanks!" Shaggy said.

The man handed Shaggy his coat. Shaggy noticed a big letter W on the back.

"What does the W stand for?" asked Shaggy.

"Woodruff. As in the 'Amazing Woodruff,'" Eudora answered as she headed over with Daphne. She gave the man a kiss on the cheek. "To be honest, I didn't think you'd show up. I thought you'd still be angry."

"About what?" Daphne asked.

"Oh, nothing," Woodruff said.

"It's time I set the record straight," Eudora said. "I was Woodruff's assistant many years ago. And during his act, I accidentally messed up one of his tricks. I still feel responsible for what happened to your career."

"Like, what happened, man?" Shaggy asked.

"Well, young man, let me put it this way," Woodruff said. "Before this evening, had you ever heard of the Amazing Woodruff?"

"I don't think so," Shaggy said. "How about you, Scoob?"

Scooby shook his head.

"Well, enough of this chitchat," Eudora interrupted. "The show will be starting soon. Why don't you go inside, Woodruff? I need to check on our other guests. And don't forget your next assignment, Daphne." Eudora and the Amazing Woodruff walked away.

"Raggy, rat's ris?" Scooby asked. He pointed with his paw at a bowl of numbered tags.

20

"I don't know, Scoob," Shaggy said. "But they look like the numbers we use when we're waiting in line at the bakery."

"Shaggy, those are the numbered claim checks you're supposed to give the guests," Daphne said. "Now how are you going to know whose coat is whose?"

"Like, no problem, Daph," Shaggy said. "So far, only a couple of people have checked their coats. You keep an eye on things in here and we'll be right back."

Chapter 4

Shaggy carried the bowl of claim checks into the grand ballroom. More guests had arrived and they were all mingling and talking. Shaggy and Scooby looked around for Muldoon the Magnificent and the Amazing Woodruff. They wanted to give them their claim checks.

Then Scooby sniffed the air hungrily. His nose had caught some kind of scent.

"Ris ray, Raggy," Scooby said. "Rood!"

Scooby held his nose high and led Shaggy around the ballroom. He stopped in front of a picture of a magician's banquet.

"Scoob, I think your nose is seeing things," Shaggy said. "This is just a picture of some people eating."

The picture suddenly rolled up into the ceiling. A man dressed in a white jacket and black bow tie walked through. He was carrying a tray of food.

"As my grandfather always used to say," said Shaggy, "where there's food, there's a kitchen. Let's go, Scooby-Doo."

Shaggy and Scooby walked down the hallway. Just ahead, they saw a figure standing in the shadows.

"Stand aside, Scoob," Shaggy whispered. "That must be another waiter. Let's get in position to grab a snack from his tray as he walks by."

The figure got closer and Shaggy and Scooby saw that it wasn't a waiter. It was someone dressed all in black, wearing a black mask with green feathers.

"Prepare yourselves, my friends, for a magic show you will never, ever forget," he whispered. "When the Masked Magician is finished, you'll wish you'd never come here tonight."

The masked man laughed as he turned and ran back into the shadows.

"I don't know about you, Scoob, but I don't have to wait for anyone to finish to wish I'd never come here tonight," Shaggy said. "Let's get out of here."

"Right!" Scooby barked. They turned and ran back into the ballroom.

"Hold on, you two," a voice called. Shaggy and Scooby turned around and saw Fred and Velma standing there. "And just where do you two think you're going?" Velma asked.

Before Shaggy could answer, a man dressed in a rumpled black suit approached from the same direction where the Masked Magician had disappeared.

"We're running away from him," Shaggy said. "He's the Masked Magician."

"No, he's not," Fred said. "He's Stan Quackenbush, the president of the Magicians' Club."

"Mr. Quackenbush!" Velma called. Stan saw Velma and came over to say hello.

"Did you find what you were looking for?" asked Velma.

"Absolutely," Stan replied. "Thank you for your help. I thought I would never find the meeting."

"What meeting?" Fred asked.

"The Magicians' Club had an emergency meeting here tonight," Stan replied. "There are rumors that Eudora Pillbox has been breaking the magician's code by revealing the secrets to some of our magic tricks." Stan rubbed his nose. "This is very serious business. The club has authorized me to take any steps necessary to make sure Eudora stops what she's doing." Stan's face twisted up and then let out a giant sneeze. "*Ah-ah-ah-choo!*"

"Are you all right?" Fred asked.

"Yes, yes, I'm — *AH-CHOOOOO!*" Stan sneezed. "I'm just very allergic to all kinds of fur. Including dog hair."

"Ruh?" Scooby said.

"Like, don't sweat it," Shaggy said. "Scooby and I will go see how Daphne's doing in the coatroom. I think Eudora had another job for her, anyway."

"You left Daphne alone in the coatroom?" Fred asked.

"Relax, Fred, my man," Shaggy said. "All she has to do is hand out the little numbered claim checks."

"You mean the ones you're holding in your hands?" asked Velma.

Shaggy looked down at the bowl of claim checks.

"Boy, we really did it this time, Scoob," Shaggy said. "Let's go help Daphne before it's too late."

But before Shaggy and Scooby could turn to go, Eudora Pillbox's voice filled the ballroom.

"Ladies and gentlemen," Eudora said, "please welcome the Masked Magician!"

"You know, Scoob, I think we're already too late," Shaggy whispered.

Chapter 5

Fred, Velma, Scooby, and Shaggy joined the crowd in the ballroom as the show began. One wall of the room magically disappeared. A stage that was empty except for a tall black box stood in its place.

"Jinkies!" Velma said. "That's a really neat trick."

"I thought you didn't believe in magic," Shaggy said.

"I don't. Something can be a trick without being magic, Shaggy," Velma explained.

A tall man dressed in a black suit and a black mask walked onto the stage. Everyone in the ballroom started clapping. The Masked Magician held up one hand to stop the applause.

"Good evening, ladies and gentlemen," the magician said. "It is an honor to join you this evening in support of our favorite charity. I promised Eudora a show she would never forget. So let's get to it. Please welcome my assistant for this evening's performance."

The Masked Magician clapped his hands and motioned for someone to join him onstage.

"Daphne!" Fred, Velma, Shaggy, and Scooby exclaimed.

Everyone watched as Daphne walked onto the stage. She was still wearing her black dress, only now she had a red scarf tied around her neck, too.

"Like, I didn't know Daphne could do magic," Shaggy said.

"Me, neither," echoed Fred.

The Masked Magician opened a big black

box. He showed that it was empty. Then he helped Daphne step in and closed the front of the box.

"Watch closely," he said. He snapped his fingers and tiny sparks jumped off his fingertips. Then he opened the door of the box.

"Rhere's Raphne?" Scooby barked.

The box looked empty. The Masked Magician reached in and took out a white rabbit. It was wearing a red scarf around its neck.

"Man, now I've seen everything!" Shaggy said. "That guy just turned Daphne into a rabbit."

"No, he didn't, Shaggy," Velma said. "It's just a trick with a logical explanation."

"I sure hope so," Shaggy said. "Otherwise, we're going to have to keep a lot of carrots in the back of the Mystery Machine."

The Masked Magician put the rabbit back into the box. He closed the door, flicked more sparks at the box, then opened the door again. Daphne stepped out. Everyone in the ballroom applauded.

"And now, for my next trick, I would like to invite our gracious hostess onstage," the magician said.

The Masked Magician motioned to the other side of the stage. This time, Eudora stepped up. Her necklace glittered in the spotlight. All of the guests applauded again.

The Masked Magician helped Eudora into the black box. He closed the door and once again shot sparks off his fingers.

When he opened the door, he pulled out

the rabbit again. But this time, it was wearing Eudora's expensive diamond necklace. The magician held the rabbit's face up to his ear.

"What's that?" he asked the rabbit. He pretended to listen to it.

"Eudora would like everyone to know that after my last trick, dinner will be served in the main dining room," he said. "And now, the moment you've all been waiting for."

The Masked Magician stepped into the black box himself, carrying the rabbit with him. The box started spinning around and around, faster and faster. Suddenly it stopped, and Eudora tumbled out onto the stage, holding the rabbit.

Everyone clapped wildly as they headed toward the dining room for dinner. Onstage, Eudora was still dizzy from the spinning box, so Daphne helped steady her. Fred, Velma, Shaggy, and Scooby ran up to the stage.

"Like, you were terrific, Daph," Shaggy said. "Scoob and I want to know what happened to you inside that box."

"I want to know what happened to the Masked Magician," Daphne said, looking around.

"And I want to know what happened to

that diamond necklace," Velma said. "Because the rabbit isn't wearing it anymore."

Eudora felt her neck. "And neither am I!" she exclaimed.

"Gang, it looks like we have a mystery to solve," Fred declared.

Chapter 6

"I'm really not feeling well, kids," Eudora said. "I'm going to go lie down for a while. You've got to find that necklace before the big auction. If not, the benefit will be ruined, and so will my reputation."

"You can count on us," Fred said.

Eudora slowly walked off the stage and went to her office. She looked worried and upset. The gang gathered around the mysterious black box.

"We'd better split up to look for clues," Velma said.

"Velma's right," Fred agreed. "Daphne and I will start here."

"Shaggy, Scooby, and I will check out the other rooms and see if we can find the magician," Velma said. "Let's go, fellas. Shaggy? Scooby?"

Velma looked around and saw Shaggy and Scooby playing with the magician's magic wand.

"This is no time for fooling around, you two," Velma said. "We have to go look for clues."

Shaggy and Scooby were having a tug-of-war with the magic wand. Suddenly it broke

with a loud snap, sending Shaggy and Scooby tumbling across the stage in different directions. Scooby bumped into Daphne, knocking her into the black box. The front panel slammed shut behind her.

"Rorry, Raphne," Scooby said. He reached over with his paw to open the panel. But it seemed to be stuck. Scooby stood on his hind legs and tried to pry open the door with his front paws. Instead, he lost his balance and knocked into it again. The box started spinning around and around. Fred rushed over, stopped it, and opened the door. The box was empty!

"Zoinks!" Shaggy exclaimed. "See what you've done, Scooby? Like, you made Daphne disappear."

"Ruh?" Scooby said.

"I'll stay here to look for Daphne," Fred said. "She's probably caught behind a secret panel or something. Velma, why don't you take Shaggy and Scooby with you and look around the other rooms."

Velma led Shaggy and Scooby off the stage and out of the ballroom. Their first stop was the coatroom.

"I'll look out in the hallway," Velma said. "You two check in there."

Shaggy and Scooby looked around the coatroom. There were a lot more coats than when they'd left. They started patting down each coat on its hanger. Then Shaggy heard a crunching sound coming from Scooby's direction.

"Scooby, what are you eating?" Shaggy asked.

"Rarrots," Scooby answered.

"Like, where did you find carrots?"

"Rin ris," Scooby replied. He held up a

cape with the initials *MM* stitched into it.

"MM," Shaggy read. "Hmm, I think that's Muldoon the Magnificent's cape. But why would he have carrots in his pocket?"

"Ror rabbits?" Scooby barked.

"Rabbits? Like, Scoob, I think we just found a genuine clue," Shaggy said with amazement. "The Masked Magician used a rabbit in his act. And his initials also happen to be MM Scooby, old pal, I think we've just solved the mystery. Come on, let's go tell Velma."

Shaggy nudged Scooby out of the coatroom before he could even finish his carrot.

They headed back down the hallway. But this time they didn't end up in the ballroom. Instead, they found themselves in a room that looked like a library.

"I think we took the wrong hallway, Scoob. Let's go back to the coatroom and start again," Shaggy said.

They turned to leave the room. But there, standing right in front of them, was the Masked Magician!

"Rikes!" Scooby yelped.

"Run, Scooby!" Shaggy yelled. "Run!"

Chapter 7

The magician glared at Shaggy and Scooby through his black mask. He raised his hands into the air, waved them around mysteriously, and then flicked his fingers at Shaggy and Scooby. Sparks leaped from his fingertips. Shaggy and Scooby watched as the sparks hit a statue, which disappeared in a cloud of smoke. In its place sat a white rabbit.

"Quick, Scoob, let's hop on out of here," Shaggy called. He and Scooby ran into the next room and jumped up onto a large table. The top of the table folded in two and the table became a giant chair.

"Just our luck, Scoob," Shaggy sighed. "We found a room that does its own magic tricks. Throw something big on the floor to block his way."

"Rokay," Scooby said. He noticed an enormous floor lamp next to the doorway. He knocked it over to block the door. But as soon as it hit the floor, it turned into a bouquet of flowers.

"Like, this is no time to give him presents, Scoob," Shaggy said. He spied a tall cabinet in the corner. He ran over and opened it. "Quick, Scoob, in here," Shaggy said.

The two friends jumped inside and closed the door tightly. They heard the Masked Magician walk into the room.

"You can't hide from the Masked Magician," his voice said eerily.

"Scoob, get your paw out of my back," Shaggy whispered.

"Ri rant," Scooby answered.

"*Shhhhh*," Shaggy warned. "He'll hear us."

Suddenly, they felt something thump the front of the cabinet.

"Ah, I knew I'd find you," the Masked Magician whispered. "Now for one of my favorite magic tricks: the disappearing cabinet."

"What are we going to do, Scoob?" Shaggy asked. "Like, I'm too young to disappear."

"One," the Masked Magician counted.

"Maybe if we scrunch up really small, his magic powers will miss us," Shaggy said. "Get ready to scrunch, Scooby."

"Two," said the magician. "Three!"

"Scrunch!" Shaggy yelled.

"Runch!" Scooby barked.

The next thing Scooby and Shaggy knew, they felt the back of the cabinet give way. Suddenly, they were tumbling across the stage.

"Shaggy, Scooby, where have you been?" Velma asked. "I looked for you in the coatroom but you weren't there."

"Like, sorry, Velma," Shaggy said. "But we were a little busy being chased by the Masked Magician. He almost turned us into rabbits!"

Fred and Velma looked at each other and then back at Shaggy and Scooby.

"It's true," Shaggy said. "Right, Scoob?"

Scooby nodded.

"Like, we saw with our own eyes how he shot sparks from his fingertips and changed a statue into a rabbit," Shaggy explained. "Like this."

Scooby posed and pretended to be a statue. Shaggy held up his fingers and pretended to zap Scooby. Scooby started hopping around like a bunny.

"Would you two knock it off?" Fred said. "We still have to find Daphne."

"Then why don't you look over here?" Daphne asked. The rest of the gang turned and saw their missing friend standing in one of the doorways.

"Daphne!" they all shouted, gathering around her. "Are you all right?"

"I'm fine," she said. "When Scooby knocked me into the box, I thought I was going back into the secret compartment."

"Like, you mean the cabinet we hid in?" Shaggy asked.

"Right," Daphne said.

"But when the box started spinning," Velma interrupted, "you were lowered on a platform that went under the stage."

"That's right," gasped Daphne. "How did you know?"

"It's all perfectly logical," Velma said.

"When I was under the stage, I heard some voices through the floorboards," Daphne continued. "I followed the voices and came out in this hallway by the kitchen. But only after I found a clue that I think will help us solve this mystery."

Daphne held out her hand.

"Like, that's just a cuff link with the letter *M* on it," Shaggy said.

"And that's all we need to see to solve this mystery," Fred said. "Gang, it's definitely time to set a trap."

Chapter 8

"Here's the plan," Fred began. "We're going to trap the Masked Magician with his own magic."

"Sounds great, Fred," Shaggy said. "But how are we gonna do that?"

"That's where you and Scooby come in," Velma said.

"No, that's where Scooby and I get out," Shaggy replied. "As in out the front door of this creepy place."

"But we need Scooby to pretend to be the greatest magician in the world," Velma said.

"That's our best chance of luring the Masked Magician out."

"What do you say, Scooby?" Daphne asked. "We'll give you a big cape and everything."

"Ruh-ruh," Scooby barked.

"How about if we throw in a magic wand?" Fred suggested.

Scooby shook his head back and forth.

"And a couple of Scooby Snacks?" Velma added.

Scooby thought for exactly two seconds. "Rokay!" he barked. Velma tossed the two Scooby Snacks into the air. Scooby jumped up and gobbled them down.

"Shaggy and I will hide in the secret cabinet that leads to the black box," Fred explained. "When I

give the signal, Scooby, you get the Masked Magician to step into the box. Shaggy and I will jump out and capture him."

"I'll go to the coatroom and find a cape we can borrow," Daphne said.

"And I'll go find Eudora and tell her our plan," Velma said. "I'll ask her to spread the word about our challenger to the Masked Magician. But we need a convincing magician's name."

Everyone looked at one another for a minute and tried to think of a good name.

"Like, I got it!" Shaggy exclaimed. "Ladies and gentlemen, meet Hairy Scoobdini!"

"I like it!" Daphne said with a smile. She and Velma went to take care of their assignments.

"Now, remember, Scooby," Fred said. "You want to get the Masked Magician to step into the magic box, got it?"

"Rot rit!" barked Scooby.

Fred and Shaggy left the stage to take

their positions in the other room. Daphne returned, carrying a long black cape. She tied it around Scooby's neck.

"Ranks," barked Scooby.

"I'm going to meet up with Velma and Eudora," Daphne said. "Good luck, Scoobdini." She kissed Scooby on the nose and ran off the stage.

Scooby wrapped himself in the giant cape. He walked around the stage and pretended to be a real magician. He bowed to his imaginary audience. Then he held up a paw to stop the pretend applause.

Scooby reached into his cape and pulled out a bouquet of flowers. This time, he heard some real applause. He looked at the other side of the stage. The Masked Magician stood there, clapping.

"Great trick," he said. "Now I'll show you a great trick. Let me show you how I turn a dog into a rabbit!"

The Masked Magician walked slowly toward Scooby. As he walked, the magician raised his hands to fling his magical sparks at Scooby.

"Rikes!" barked Scooby. The Masked Magician got closer. Scooby took a deep breath, closed his eyes, and ran right at him. Just as the Masked Magician was about to grab him, Scooby jumped

into the black box. His tail slammed the door
behind him.

Shaggy and Fred opened the secret door
inside the cabinet on the other side.

"Scooby!" Shaggy exclaimed. "Where's
the Masked Magician?"

Just then, the Masked Magician opened
the front of the black box. Scooby started to
run out through the cabinet. The Masked
Magician reached out and grabbed Scooby's
cape. He gave the cape a hard tug, expecting

to pull Scooby back. Instead, the cape snapped in half, sending the Masked Magician flying backward.

Shaggy, Fred, and Scooby peered through the back of the black box. There, onstage, sat the Masked Magician, completely covered in flowers.

Chapter 9

F red, Shaggy, and Scooby gathered around the Masked Magician. Velma and Daphne came into the room with Eudora.

"Jinkies!" Velma exclaimed. "We didn't even start telling anyone about the great Scoobdini and you've already captured the Masked Magician."

"Well, Eudora," Fred asked, "would you like to unmask the Masked Magician and see who really stole your diamond necklace?"

"Absolutely," Eudora said. She walked up onto the stage and stood next to the Masked Magician. She reached over and pulled off his mask.

"Woodruff!" Eudora cried.

"Just as we suspected," Velma said.

"But how did you know?" Eudora asked.

"At first, we weren't completely sure," Daphne said. "We thought initially it was Stan Quackenbush."

"Stan? From the Magicians' Club?" Eudora asked. "Why would he want to do something like this?"

"To stop you from telling magicians' secrets," Fred said.

"But I haven't told any magicians' secrets," Eudora said with surprise.

"I know, Eudora," Stan said. He stood by the doorway to the dining room. "The Magicians' Club sometimes gets carried away.

They take themselves very seriously. All I was going to do was talk to you."

"We knew for sure he wasn't involved because the Masked Magician used rabbits in his act," Velma explained. "And Stan's very allergic to animal fur."

"Besides," Stan added, "I'd never use magic for something bad. That goes against everything we stand for as magicians."

Stan paused, then sneezed twice.

"Resundheit!" Scooby said.

"Our next suspect was Muldoon the Magnificent," Daphne said. "He was pretty upset about your canceling the TV special he planned for tonight's benefit."

"But I asked him to perform live," Eudora said.

"Didn't you know that Muldoon has stage

fright?" Stan asked. "He only performs on television."

"Oh, dear, I had no idea," Eudora said.

"What about those carrots Scooby found in his coat?" Shaggy asked.

"Woodruff planted them there," Fred said. "To make us suspect Muldoon. Just like he hoped we would when we found this." Fred showed Eudora the silver cuff link.

"Is this Muldoon's?" she asked.

"You're looking at it upside down," Velma said. "What letter do you see when you look at it the right way?"

Eudora bent her neck and looked at the cuff link upside down.

"Why, it's a *W*," she exclaimed. "For Woodruff." She turned to confront him. "But why did you do all this?"

Everyone looked at the Amazing Woodruff.

"I've been angry at you ever since you ruined my act all those years ago," Woodruff said angrily. "Because of you, I never became the great magician I should have been. So tonight I pretended to be the Masked Magician so I could ruin your career like you ruined mine. I was going to sell the necklace and use the money to build my own magic palace dedicated to the Amazing Woodruff. And my plan would've worked, too, if it weren't for those kids and their meddling mutt."

"I'd better call the police," Eudora said. "And then I should get back to my guests. We still have the auction to do."

"Aren't you forgetting something, Eudora?" Stan asked. He reached his hand out to Woodruff. Woodruff grumbled as he reached into his costume and took out the necklace. He handed it to Stan, who fastened it back around Eudora's neck.

"Thank you, Stan. And as for you," Eudora said to Scooby, "how can I ever thank you?"

"Like, I have an idea," Shaggy said. He ran over and whispered something to Eudora and Stan.

"Great idea," Stan said. "I'll be right back." He ran out of the room.

"Ladies and gentlemen, and especially dogs," Eudora announced. "It is my pleasure to present, in his first live performance, Muldoon the Magnificent."

Muldoon walked into the room with Stan. He bowed as Eudora and the gang clapped.

"And now, a most special trick for a most special dog," Muldoon said. He took a red silk handkerchief from his coat pocket. He started unfolding it and unfolding it and unfolding it and unfolding it until it was as large as a bedsheet. Stan took one side and Eudora took the other. They held up the sheet so it looked like a red wall. Muldoon gestured dramatically. He stood right in front of the sheet.

"Please join me," he said. "One . . ."

"Two," everyone counted. "Three!"

Muldoon grabbed the center of the sheet and yanked it away from Stan and Eudora. A huge twelve-course meal had appeared.

"Now that's one magic trick you can really sink your teeth into," Shaggy called.

"Scooby-Dooby-Doo!" Scooby barked happily.

Solve a Mystery with Scooby-Doo!

SCOOBY-DOO! MYSTERIES

by James Gelsey

Ruh-roh!

Read them all!

Zoinks!

$3.99 each!

- ☐ BDE 0-590-81909-7   #1: SCOOBY-DOO AND THE HAUNTED CASTLE
- ☐ BDE 0-590-81910-0   #2: SCOOBY-DOO AND THE MUMMY'S CURSE
- ☐ BDE 0-590-81914-3   #3: SCOOBY-DOO AND THE SNOW MONSTER
- ☐ BDE 0-590-81917-8   #4: SCOOBY-DOO AND THE SUNKEN SHIP
- ☐ BDE 0-439-08095-9   #5: SCOOBY-DOO AND THE HOWLING WOLFMAN
- ☐ BDE 0-439-08278-1   #6: SCOOBY-DOO AND THE VAMPIRE'S REVENGE
- ☐ BDE 0-439-11346-6   #7: SCOOBY-DOO AND THE CARNIVAL CREEPER
- ☐ BDE 0-439-11347-4   #8: SCOOBY-DOO AND THE GROOVY GHOST
- ☐ BDE 0-439-11348-2   #9: SCOOBY-DOO AND THE ZOMBIE'S TREASURE
- ☐ BDE 0-439-11349-0   #10: SCOOBY-DOO AND THE SPOOKY STRIKEOUT
- ☐ BDE 0-439-10664-8   #11: SCOOBY-DOO AND THE FAIRGROUND PHANTOM
- ☐ BDE 0-439-18876-8   #12: SCOOBY-DOO AND THE FRANKENSTEIN MONSTER
- ☐ BDE 0-439-18877-6   #13: SCOOBY-DOO AND THE RUNAWAY ROBOT
- ☐ BDE 0-439-18878-4   #14: SCOOBY-DOO AND THE MASKED MAGICIAN

At bookstores everywhere!

Scholastic Inc., P.O. Box 7502, Jefferson City, MO 65102

Please send me the books I have checked above. I am enclosing $_____ (please add $2.00 to cover shipping and handling). Send check or money order–no cash or C.O.D.s please.

Name_____Birthdate_____

Address_____

City_____State/Zip_____

Please allow four to six weeks for delivery. Offer good in U.S.A. only. Sorry, mail orders are not available to residents of Canada. Prices subject to change.

SCO101

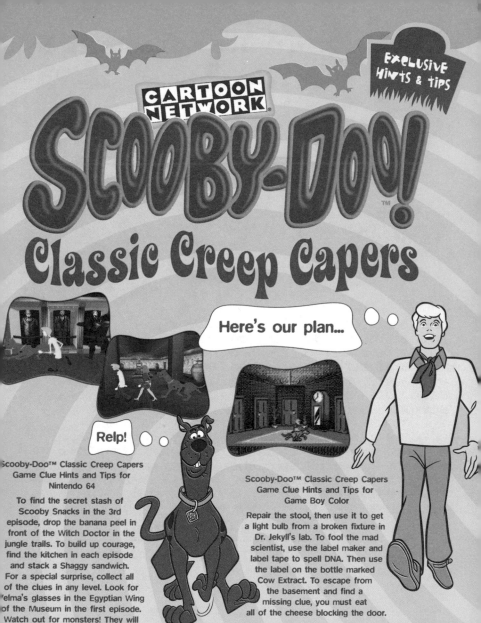

EXCLUSIVE HINTS & TIPS

CARTOON NETWORK®

SCOOBY-DOO!™

Classic Creep Capers

Here's our plan...

Relp!

Scooby-Doo™ Classic Creep Capers
Game Clue Hints and Tips for
Nintendo 64

To find the secret stash of
Scooby Snacks in the 3rd
episode, drop the banana peel in
front of the Witch Doctor in the
jungle trails. To build up courage,
find the kitchen in each episode
and stack a Shaggy sandwich.
For a special surprise, collect all
of the clues in any level. Look for
Velma's glasses in the Egyptian Wing
of the Museum in the first episode.
Watch out for monsters! They will
make your courage meter go down.

Scooby-Doo™ Classic Creep Capers
Game Clue Hints and Tips for
Game Boy Color

Repair the stool, then use it to get
a light bulb from a broken fixture in
Dr. Jekyll's lab. To fool the mad
scientist, use the label maker and
label tape to spell DNA. Then use
the label on the bottle marked
Cow Extract. To escape from
the basement and find a
missing clue, you must eat
all of the cheese blocking the door.

NINTENDO.64

coming soon